For Marc, my middle one — S.I.

This edition published by Kids Can Press in 2017
Originally published in Spanish under the title *Mediano*.

Copyright © 2015 EDICIONES LA FRAGATINA
Text © Susanna Isern
Illustrations © Manon Gauthier
English translation © 2017 Kids Can Press

Kids Can Press gratefully acknowledges the financial support of the Government
of Ontario, through the Ontario Media Development Corporation; the Ontario Arts
Council; the Canada Council for the Arts; and the Government of Canada, through
the CBF, for our publishing activity.

Published in Canada and the U.S. by Kids Can Press Ltd.
25 Dockside Drive, Toronto, ON M5A 0B5

Kids Can Press is a Corus Entertainment Inc. company

www.kidscanpress.com

The artwork in this book was rendered in cut-paper collage, pencil and mixed media.
The text is set in Archer.

English edition edited by Jennifer Stokes

Printed and bound in Shenzhen, China, in 3/2017 through Asia Pacific Offset

CM 17 0 9 8 7 6 5 4 3 2 1

Library and Archives Canada Cataloguing in Publication

Isern, Susanna
[Mediano. English]

       Middle bear / Susanna Isern ; illustrations, Manon Gauthier.

Translation of: Mediano.
ISBN 978-1-77138-842-9 (hardcover)

       I. Gauthier, Manon, 1959–, illustrator II. Title. III. Title:
Mediano. English.

PZ7.I825Mi 2017   j863'.7   C2016-908047-1

MIDDLE BEAR

SUSANNA ISERN
MANON GAUTHIER

Kids Can Press

He had been born the second of three brothers.
He was not big, but he was not small, either.
Neither strong nor weak, neither tall nor short,
neither a lot nor a little ...
    He was the middle one.

Everything around him was made
to his size. He had a middle-sized
bicycle, a middle-sized umbrella
and middle-sized clothes. He
played with middle-sized cars.

When he went fishing with his middle-sized fishing rod,
he managed to catch the most middle-sized fish in the lake,
which he put into his middle-sized basket.

When he got home, his parents would cook the fish. He ate his off a middle-sized plate, in middle-sized mouthfuls, and drank half a glass of water.

After supper, he went to his middle-sized bed
and counted stars, all of them middle-sized.
(He always went to bed before his older brother
and after his younger one.)

In the afternoons, his father would often go out
with his older brother to gather walnuts and almonds,
while his mother would nap with his younger brother.
That's when he would read himself a story.
A middle-sized story, like this one.

Sometimes he felt sad. His tears were middle-sized, like ants, not tiny like fleas or huge like wasps. In a middle-sized voice, he told the wind:

"I don't want to be the middle one."

One morning, when he and his brothers woke up, their mother called to them from bed.

"Papa and I are ill! We need you to go and fetch some willow tree bark," she said between sneezes.

But the willow is at the top of the mountain, he thought. *And that's really high.*

He was worried, less than a lot … but more than a little.

"I know you can do it," their father encouraged them.

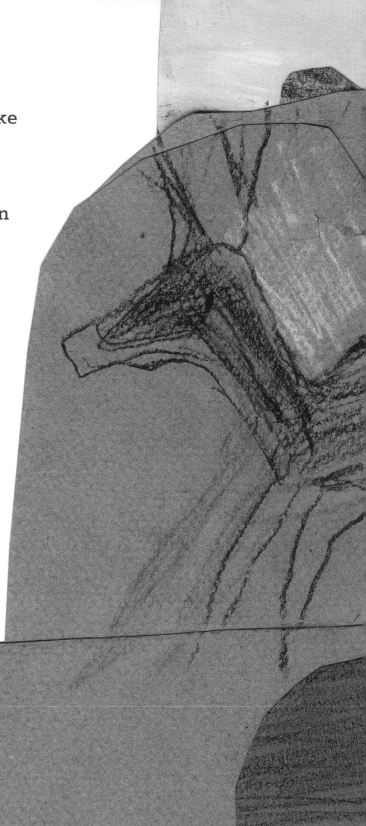

They put on their boots, picked up their backpacks and ventured into the woods in the direction of the mountain.

After walking for several hours, they were forced to stop at a partly frozen river. They could only cross it by jumping from the bank to the patch of ice on the other side.

"I will jump onto the ice and go on alone," said his older brother.

With one huge leap, he reached the frozen ledge. But he was so heavy that the ice broke, and he fell into the water.

"I am much lighter," said his younger brother. "It will be better if I go."

He took a running start and then jumped. But his legs were so little that he didn't reach the ice. He sank into the water and had to be rescued by his brothers.

Soaked and shivering, his brothers turned to him.
"You will have to try," they said.

He considered the problem. *The gap is very wide,*
he thought, *and the ice is very thin. If my brothers
were middle-sized, like me, they might have made it
to the other side ...*

Then, although he was only half convinced, he closed his middle-sized eyes and, with his middle-sized legs, he jumped. His jump, which was middle-sized, was enough to reach the ice. And his weight, which was only middling, did not break it. He straightened his middle-sized feet, stretched out his middle-sized arms and glided over the ice to the shore.

As incredible as it seemed, he had done it.
Because he was the middle one.

He looked back. His brothers were cheering from the other side of the river. He had to go on alone, but he did not mind. He walked to the foot of the huge mountain, the biggest and highest of all. He took a medium breath and began to climb at a middling speed.

With one middle-sized step after the other, he reached the top.

The willow tree was not as he had imagined it. All around him were big trees almost double his size and small trees that did not even reach his height. The willow was middle-sized, just like him. Yet this tree was special — it could cure things!

At that moment, he was overcome with pride. He cut a middle-sized piece of bark, put it in his middle-sized backpack and, with one middle-sized step after the other, made his way back down the mountain.

At home, his parents were waiting under their blankets.
Despite being ill, they ran outside to give him a hug.

He was not big, but he was not small, either. Neither strong
nor weak, neither tall nor short, neither a lot nor a little ...
   He was the middle one.
   And being the middle one, he could do all sorts of things:
small things, middle-sized things and big things, too.